I Like to Read® books, created by award-winning
picture book artists as well as talented newcomers,
instill confidence and the joy of reading in new readers.

We want to hear every new reader say, "I like to read!"

Visit our website for flash cards, activities, and more about the series:
www.holidayhouse.com/I-Like-to-Read/
#ILTR
This book has been tested by an educational expert
and determined to be a guided reading level A.

To our cat, Bailey,
aka Kit-T, aka Skunk,
the best cat
on the planet

I LIKE TO READ is a registered trademark of Holiday House, Inc.
Copyright © 2016 by Ethan Long
All Rights Reserved
HOLIDAY HOUSE is registered in the U.S. Patent and Trademark Office.
Printed and bound in April 2017 at Hong Kong Graphics and Printing Ltd., China.
The artwork was created digitally.
www.holidayhouse.com
3 5 7 9 10 8 6 4 2

Library of Congress Cataloging-in-Publication Data
Long, Ethan, author, illustrator.
Big Cat / by Ethan Long. — First edition.
pages cm. — (I like to read)
Summary: A hefty feline puts up with all kinds of indignities
from the children in her loving but rambunctious family.
ISBN 978-0-8234-3538-8 (hardcover)
[1. Cats—Fiction. 2. Family life—Fiction.] I. Title.
PZ7.L8453Bi 2016
[E]—dc23
2015014875

ISBN 978-0-8234-3881-5 (paperback)

BIG CAT

by **Ethan Long**

I Like to Read

HOLIDAY HOUSE • NEW YORK

Big Cat can nap.

Big Cat can wake.

Big Cat can hug.

Big Cat can fly.

Big Cat can hide.

Big Cat can dance.

Big Cat can be fun.

Big Cat can sit.

Big Cat can see.

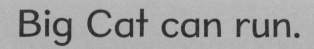

Big Cat can run.

Big Cat can be fun.

I Like to Read®

Visit http://www.holidayhouse.com/I-Like-to-Read/ for more about I Like to Read®
books, including flash cards, reproducibles, and the complete list of titles.